If These Walls Could Talk
Anna's Revival
Part 4

By: Ricky St. Julien II

ISBN- 9798560092511

Book Production: Crystell Publications
You're The Publisher, We're Your Legs
We Help You Self Publish Your Book

BOP E-mail ONLY – cleva@crystalstell.com
E-Mail – minkassitant@yahoo.com
Website: www.crystellpublications.com
(405) 414-3991

Printed in the USA

DEDICATION

I dedicate this book to you. Yes, you the reader. If you have made it this far in this series by reading the previous books, you're the real MVP. Thanks for following me in this journey to success and flipping through all the pages of entertainment along the way as I have painted the picture of the lives of these characters on paper. Stay tuned for more.

PREFACE

Lil Riley jammed the pool stick up Losstin's asshole and started violating his anus with the pool stick.

"Upstairs!" cried Losstin "Under the bed in the master bedroom upstairs. It's all there! I swear! Just, please stop!"

"Fuck you pig! You better not be lying. I'm still doing this to you though for giving me a hard time and in memory of my homeboys you killed on the highway."

Lil Riley continued shoving the pool stick up the Detective's ass. "Love it! Love it! Feel it! Feel it!" He growled like a mad man.

Anna was looking at Lil Riley scared to death. She knew he was crazy, but she hadn't seen him that angry in years. The last time she saw him that angry was when they first met and he whipped her with a belt and shoved his fist in her pussy. She was frightened, but getting turned on at the same time. Detective Losstin passed out from the pain and Lil Riley ran upstairs to the master bedroom. He looked under the bed and found $200,000 dollars and five kilos of cocaine. He grabbed the duffel bags of money and dope and ran back downstairs. Anna was kneeling over Detective Losstin obviously feeling sorry for him and trying to nurse him back to consciousness. Lil Riley knew he had mentally fucked her up forever. She had seen and knew too much. He grabbed her and hugged her as tight as he could.

"I'm sorry Anna," he said.

"Sorry for what Daddy?"

"For this."

"BOOM!"

Lil Riley lifted his .38 cal and shot Anna in the head. He then walked over to Detective Losstin and let two shots go into the back of his head. Lil Riley walked out the house the same way he went in and escaped into the darkness.

If These Walls Could Talk
Anna's Revival
Part 4

CHAPTER 1

"Stop it Daddy! Please stop!" cried Anna

Nine-year-old Anna Davis lay down with her tiny body frozen against the mattress as her father came into her room and took advantage of her inexperienced body. Her mother was a waitress working graveyard shifts at a nearby diner to help support her family. Her father was a Colonel in the army who stayed away most of the time, but when he was home, he had a bad habit of getting drunk and making a routine of molesting poor Anna while her mother was away at work.

"Shhhh! Don't cry Daddy's girl. Be a good little girl for Daddy!"

Anna did her best to push her father off of her, but his body weight was too heavy to fight against as he lay on top of her and violated her innocent body. Anna cried like a baby as it felt as though her body was being ripped apart and she was robbed of her virginity by her own father. He huffed and puffed on top of her until he reached his climax and pulled up his pants and walked out the room like what just did was a normal ritual between a father and daughter. He walked into the kitchen and grabbed a pint of Blue Bell ice cream from the freezer and went sat in the living room in front of the television.

"Anna! Come here girl!" He yelled from the living room.

Anna got out of the bed and limped into the living room sniffling as her father picked her up and placed her on his lap feeding her ice cream to make her feel better as they watched late night episodes of Jay Leno. When Anna's mother would get home from work, she would see Anna asleep on her father's chest as she pictured him as a loyal husband and loving father to his one and only daughter completely unaware of his horrendous acts. Anna could never understand how could the man that was supposed to provide for her and protect her from the world do the gruesome things he did to her and inflict so much pain.

Weeks went by and weeks turned into months as months turned into years with Anna experiencing the acts of molestation from her father. She was now eleven years old and still had never told anybody her father's dirty little secret in fear of embarrassment and being hurt even more by her father. Her tiny body had now started to experience the early stages of puberty as her nipples began to poke out and peach fuzz developed on her private areas. The trips to her bedroom from her father began to be more frequent with every stage of puberty until one day an event happened that would change that forever. Anna could hear her mother in the kitchen crying as she walked in and saw her hanging up the telephone.

"What's wrong Mommy? Why are you crying?" asked Anna.

"Come here baby," said her mother as she hugged her sobbing between tears. "It's your father Anna. He just had a terrible car accident. He didn't make it baby. Daddy is dead."

Anna couldn't understand why her mother was crying so hard.

In her mind, her mother had just delivered the best news she had heard all of her life. The only reason Anna didn't smile is because she felt sorry for her mother.

CHAPTER 2

The only thing Anna could see was a bright light after her longtime boyfriend and pimp Lil Riley shot her point blank range in the head. Lil Riley had gone crazy. The pressure of the streets and living his life in the fast lane had pushed him to his breaking point. Anna feared Lil Riley, but the love she had for him was undeniable. She would've never expected Lil Riley would blow a mental fuse and attempt to kill her for reasons that would always be unknown to her. Anna stared into the bright light in front of her and began to walk towards it. As she began to have an outer body experience, she could see herself as a little girl again walking into the light as she saw her father signaling for her to come closer. The closer she got to the light the more she could see her father's face. She stopped walking towards the light and began to run away from it.

The room was freezing cold and smelled like latex as Anna barely opened her eyes in the recovery room of the hospital and saw doctors all around her checking her vital signs. Her head was pounding as if the Energizer bunny was running around in it having a concert. Tears began to flow down her face as she realized her condition wasn't just a nightmare, but her reality.

"Doctor we have a pulse!" said a pretty Asian nurse on side of Anna.

"Awesome!" The doctor said as he shined a pin light into her pupils, Anna quickly dozed off into what she thought was a deep sleep as she started to dream about her first encounter with Lil Riley, but would later find out that her deep, sleep was really a short coma.

It was a Friday night football game, and the bleachers were full as the West Orange Stark Mustangs battled the La Porte Tigers for the 5A State Championship at NRG stadium in Houston, TX. Anna was in her senior year of high school and was the cheerleading captain with a body of a goddess at only eighteen years old.

Her hourglass shape, blonde hair and deep-sea blue eyes made her drop dead gorgeous and hard for any young man to resist with her outgoing and fun personality. Wearing her silver, blue and white team colored uniform made her look more like a Dallas Cowboy cheerleader than a high school senior.

While most of the men had their eyes on the football game, Lil Riley Price who was a hard-core drug dealer and part time pimp had his focus on Anna and her assets. Lil Riley sat back in the cut like a roaring lion seeking his prey and took advantage of the first opportunity to approach Anna as soon as he saw her walking to the concession stand. As soon as Anna turned around from buying some skittles and a Dr. Pepper, she came face to face with the most handsome young black man she ever laid eyes on. Before Lil Riley even spoke a word, Anna was already feeling love at first sight as she inhaled the scent of his Issey Miyake cologne and drew attraction to his expensive jewelry and choice of expensive clothing matching the latest pair of new Jordan's he had on his feet.

"Wussup?" said Lil Riley

"What's up?" she responded trying to sound hip.

"You wussup girl. I been watching you all night. I never saw a white girl with an ass that fine. Are you 100% white or do you have some black in you?"

"Noooo I don't have any black in me," Anna blushed.

"Do you want some?" Lil Riley asked as he grabbed his dick.

Anna couldn't help but giggle as Lil Riley fed her more and more bullshit until he finally got her phone number. Anna had always fantasized about having sex with a black guy and Lil Riley happened to pop into her life at a time when her vagina was becoming hotter and hotter with each day passing desiring a need to be satisfied. Day after day, Lil Riley filled Anna's head up with fantasies and illusions as he acted as a father figure and fucked her like a porno star.

It wasn't long until Anna was completely hooked and loyal to Lil Riley as she became submissive to him and he began pimping her over the internet selling pussy like fireworks on the 4th of July.

When Anna awoke, there was a uniformed police officer on side of her bed with a detective in a suit holding a pen and notepad.

"Hello Ms. Davis," said the detective. "I'm Detective Arnold with the homicide division. I'm going to let you get your rest because I know you are suffering from a great deal of pain, but I want to help you. We need to find out who did this to you. Did you see his face, and can you give us a name?"

Anna looked at the detective and whispered the name that she knew all so well as loud as she could with no hesitation as a tear fell from her eye.

"Li. Li Riley!"

CHAPTER 3

The Orange County Police department put a warrant out for Lil Riley's arrest and searched his home where he lived with his newborn son and baby mama, only to find out Lil Riley had just left the country and fled to Africa. After close surveillance of the home and wire taps of the phone at the residence, they were able to conclude that Lil Riley was killed during his visit to Nigeria. His unexpected death made the homicide department extremely satisfied, but Detective Arnold was a bit disappointed. He wouldn't be able to personally slap the cuffs on Lil Riley and bring him into custody and bring justice to the death of his partner Detective Robert Losstin. The cop Lil Riley murdered on the same night he shot Anna in the head.

After Anna was notified of Lil Riley's death, she was also relieved, but another piece of her heart that she didn't know existed was broken. Lil Riley was the only family she really had, and her life had always revolved around him since the day they met. A month later she was released from the hospital to go home to the penthouse her and Lil Riley once shared together before the unfortunate turn of events in Houston, TX. After settling in at home, she realized how screwed up her life had been and seemed to take a turn for the worse. There was only one way to describe how Anna was feeling. COLD. Her broken heart had suddenly turned into a block of ice and even though the bullet was removed from her head, she had lost a piece of her sanity that she couldn't regain and she would never be the same.

On the outside she was still beautiful as can be, but her soul was ugly as a wicked witch. Anna had inwardly become a monster. She no longer believed in God because she felt if God existed, her life wouldn't have been the way it was. If God was real, he wouldn't have let her be molested as a child or grow up without a loving father. If God was real, he wouldn't have allowed Lil Riley to shoot her in the head.

Anna looked at herself in the mirror admiring her beauty and flawless features processing her evil thoughts. It was at that moment that she came to the conclusion, she was God. In all actuality, she was the epitome of a white devil. She vowed to herself she would never fall victim to the abuse of another man again and would now be in control of her own destiny calling the shots. Rather indulge in self-pity and surrender to a sense of powerlessness, she consumed herself in egocentricity and fought for control of her life. The following day, Anna called the realtor to sell her penthouse in an attempt to rid herself from all of the memories she shared with Lil Riley and begin a new chapter in her life.

CHAPTER 4

Antonio Romanaldi was a 42-year-old Italian executive real estate agent who had been working at Remax Realty for the past 15 years. His track record for selling his clients, homes at top price was one of the best in the business. Antonio sat at his desk drinking his morning coffee emailing the latest MLS listings to his potential buyers when he heard his secretary open the door of his office.

"Excuse me Mr. Romanaldi. I have a client here to see you," said the secretary. "Bring him in," he said.

When Mr. Romanaldi looked up from his computer, he was surprised to see that the client wasn't a he, but in fact a she. Anna stood at the door of his office looking like a model who had just stepped out of the latest Macy's catalog. Mr. Romanaldi was a happily married man with a devoted loving wife of 10 years and 3 beautiful children, but that didn't stop him from admiring Anna's tall, sexy legs supported by her 6 inch heels and her perfect cleavage peeking from out of her sleeveless Elizabeth Taylor dress.

Mr. Romanaldi stood to greet Anna and accidentally spilled some of his coffee on his desk. He quickly began to wipe it up with some typing paper.

"Hello ma'am! What may I do you for? I mean...What may I do for you? He asked. "Hi. My name is Ms. Anna Davis and I'm here to place my penthouse on the market in hopes that you can get it sold for me as quick as possible."

"Well sure ma'am. Just have a seat so I can ask you a few questions."

Anna took a seat in front of Mr. Romanaldi crossing her legs and eyeing him seductively licking her teeth as he sat back down with a pen and paper to take notes.

"What's your reason for selling Ms. Davis?" He asked.

"My significant other who I shared the residence with recently died and there's too many memories in the house for me."

"Oh wow! I'm sorry to hear that. Did he die at the residence?"

"Oh no. He died at work in a construction accident a few months ago, lied Anna. She felt it wasn't any of his business.

"Where is the property located?"

"It's a penthouse in the Galleria area here in Houston. The address is 95114 Sage Rd."

"How much did you pay for it?"

"We paid $325,000 and I'm asking $350,000."

Mr. Romanaldi typed the address into his computer as he began to run the comps on the property to see what it was worth. He was already excited to sell the property knowing his 6% commission for selling the property would make his bank account a little fatter. As he began to run the comps he realized that the property had been purchased at a bad time when the market was high, but had declined over the years due to the market crash. He unconsciously started shaking his head no as he looked away from his computer.

"Is there a problem?" asked Anna.

"Well I'm sorry to tell you this Ms. Davis, but I just did a comparative market analysis on your property and I noticed it was purchased at a time when the market was extremely high. Today your property is only worth $285,000 in comparison to the other homes in your area. I may be able to list it for $290,00 if it's really nice, but if it's not sold in 90 days, I would recommend dropping the price."

Anna thought about what he was saying as she intensely stared in his byes remembering she wasn't wearing any panties. She uncrossed her legs making sure to spread them wide enough to give Mr. Romanaldi a clear view of her perfectly shaven fat pussy to motivate him more. Mr. Romanaldi's eyes almost popped out of his head as he stared at what was in front of him. "How about you list it for $300,000?" said Anna

"I think I can do that," he said clearing his throat, "but I'll need to stop by this evening to take pictures."

"Please do!" said Anna as she got up to leave.

Before walking out of the office, she noticed a perfect family portrait of Mr. Romanaldi with his wife and kids and felt a sting of jealousy enter her heart as she started to devise a plan on how to come out on top.

Mr. Romanaldi watched Anna twist away as he felt his erection growing in his pants and thought about how he was going to fuck the beautiful Ms. Anna Davis and walk away with a nice commission check afterwards. What he didn't know is that Anna was thinking the same exact thing.

CHAPTER 5

Later that evening Anna walked around her penthouse with her speakers blasting B.O.B "I wanna be a billionaire" in her short bath robe boxing up all of her belongings preparing to move into a new place and start a new life. Everything that belonged to her dead pimp Lil Riley was boxed up and put in one corner to the left while she made the decision to take it to the dumpster downstairs the following morning. She could still smell the scent of Lil Riley's cologne throughout the house and couldn't wait until she finally moved. She hoped Mr. Romanaldi would be able to sell her place soon because she really needed the money.

It had been over two months since she serviced any clients as an escort and the lack of selling pussy was making her stash of cash low. Just as she was boxing up the silverware and dishes in the kitchen, she heard the doorbell ring. Anna raced to the peephole and observed Mr. Romanaldi tightening his necktie outside the door. The only thing Anna had on was her black silk robe that stopped right below her ass cheeks and a big towel blotting her hair since she had not too long got out of the shower. Anna unlocked the deadbolt on the door and welcomed Mr. Romanaldi in.

"Hi!" she said "I wasn't expecting you until later. Come in."

Mr. Romanaldi entered the house with his eyes glued to Anna's body as he stepped in with a digital camera in his hands.

"This is a very nice place you have here Ms. Davis."

"Thank you. That's exactly why I expect to get my asking price for it. May I get you anything to drink?"

"No, that's ok. I just wanted to come by and take a few pictures of the inside to post in my MLS emails I will be sending out."

Anna purposely walked in front of Mr. Romanaldi into the living room as she shook her head and made the towel fall from her hair. She quickly bent over and picked the towel up making sure that Mr. Romanldi got a good view of her pink pussy hanging from the back. Mr. Romanaldi followed behind Anna with a hard on hoping to have a little fun while on the job.

"Take as many pictures as you'd like," said Anna as she sat on the couch in front of the television closing her robe. "But only of the house," she winked.

Anna was using the art of seduction against the realtor and was doing a fine job at it as he looked at her dumbfounded. He began to walk around the penthouse taking pictures of every room until he got everything he needed. When he finished, he walked back into the living room and saw Anna lying on her back on the couch playing a game on her cell phone. Her robe was slightly open and he could see her ariolas and pussy lips peeking from out of her short silk robe.

Mr. Romanaldi couldn't fight the temptation any longer as he proceeded to make his move on Anna. He casually walked up to the side of the couch and knelt down on his knees besides Anna and began to rub on her smooth legs. Anna let out a light moan as she kept her cell phone in front of her face continuing to play her game of Candy Crush on her phone. Mr. Romanaldi slid his hands up to Anna's moneymaker and started to finger fuck her as she welcomed his hands in between her legs and squirmed on the couch with anticipation. Once Mr. Romanaldi concluded that she wasn't stopping his advances, he started to kiss between Anna's legs as she opened them apart and invited him in for dinner. Anna's pussy was so hot that he could practically feel the steam hitting him in the face as he parted her lips and began to taste her peach cobbler.

"Ohhhh!" moaned Anna

Anna grabbed the back of his head with one hand pushing his face deep into her love box while she snapped pictures of him in action with the other hand on her cell phone. Mr.Romanaldi was so into the sweetness of Anna's nectar releasing on his tongue that he never noticed her snap three good pictures of him eating her out. Once Anna snapped the pictures, she put the phone down and grabbed the back of his head with both hands and started grinding on his face.

"Mmmmmm! Mmmmmm! Mmmmmmm!" she moaned.

Mr.Romanaldi was blessed with a fat tongue from his Italian bloodline and was eating Anna like a disciple attending the last supper. Anna couldn't hold back anymore and squirted her orgasm all in the realtor's mouth. He slurped up her juices like a mad dog drinking cold water from a bucket under a desert sun. He stood up and began to unbuckle his pants. To his surprise, Anna quickly stood up wrapping her robe around her body.

"No!" she said "I'm sorry sir," but I think you should leave."

Mr. Romanaldi looked at Anna like she was crazy as he wiped the thick glaze of cum out of his eyes and from around his mouth.

"Excuse me?"

"I said No! I think you should leave. I'm sorry, but business before pleasure. Once you get this place sold for me, I'm sure we can continue this, but for now I think you should go."

Anna walked towards the door and opened it as Mr. Romanaldi followed. As bad as he wanted to just take the pussy, he knew that no meant no and he was already crossing boundaries he shouldn't have. Besides, he was feeling a little egotistical for just making Anna cum so hard. He was so grateful for being able to taste her sweet hole that he decided to leave well enough alone. He figured he'd get another chance later and when he did, he planned on beating her back in.

"O.K. Ms. Davis. You will be hearing from me soon. I'm sure I will be able to find a buyer especially for you and we will continue this later sweetheart." "I hope so," Anna smiled shutting the door behind him as he walked out.

CHAPTER 6

One week later, Mr. Romanaldi called Anna into his office saying he had a buyer, and she was clear to close. Anna raced to the office to close on the deal. Surprisingly, she walked into Mr. Romanaldi's office right while his wife Mrs. Romanaldi was getting Ready walk out.

"I'm sorry " said Anna as she walked in. "Should I wait outside?"

"Oh no Ms. Davis. Come right on in. This is my wife Mrs. Romanaldi. Honey... This is Ms. Davis. The lady who's house I just closed on."

"Hi" said Mrs. Romanaldi "How are you?"

"I'm fine. Is that Avon you're wearing Mrs. Romanaldi?"

"It sure is. How could you tell?"

"Well...I'm actually a representative for Avon and sell their products. Do you have an email address I can get before you leave? I would love to send you some recent offers and coupons we currently have if that's ok with you." "Of course. I would love that!"

Mrs. Romanaldi stood to leave and extended Anna her business card with her email address on it.

"I'll see you at home Dear," she said to her husband, "And I'll be expecting those offers Ms. Davis," she smiled to Anna as she left the office.

Anna sat in the leather chair in front of Mr. Romanaldi's desk as he handed her a check and began to fidget through some paperwork and hand her some documents to sign.

"So... how much were you able to sell my place for?" she asked "I am proud to say that I got $300,000 for it. I'm looking forward to my commission check I will be receiving and finishing what we started the other evening as pleasure now that business is out the way."

"Oh...about that commission check...I'm going to need you to deposit that into my account as well when you receive it."

"I beg your pardon?"

"Check your email bad boy."

Mr. Romanaldi opened his email messages on his computer and was in total dismay as he saw the pictures of him diving face first in Anna's pussy like he was bobbing for apples.

"What is this? Some type of sick joke?"

"Oh no. It's not a joke Mr. Romanaldi. It's insurance. I'm going to need that whole $300,000. Luckily for me, I just got Mrs. Romanaldi's email address, so unless you want your lovely wife to see you eating the pink out my pussy, I suggest you make sure I receive your commission as well. Do I make myself clear?"

Mr. Romanaldi felt like a complete fool as he stared in contempt at Anna and turned beet red in the face from embarrassment.

"I can't believe you did that," he said. "Believe it! You just make sure I receive that whole 300 grand bad boy."

Anna stood to leave and turned around to look at Mr.Romalnaldi one more time before she left.

"Oh and one more thing."

"What is it Ms.Davis?"

"Thanks for the head" she winked.

Anna twisted out of the office without one ounce of pity and continued on her way. The move she had just made was only the beginning to her new way of living the Queen Bitch lifestyle.

She immediately took the proceeds of her money

she collected after selling the penthouse and leased a nice, modest 5-bedroom house in the Westchase District of Houston between Richmond and Westheimer. As soon as she settled in, instead of posting her ads on every escort site known to man focusing back on prostitution, she did something different. She started searching the web for other prostitutes who she could place to work in her new residence which would soon become the hottest brothel in Houston known as, "Anna's Revival."

CHAPTER 7

Markus Dixon also known as "Big Black" got his name from standing '6,7" weighing 290 pounds and being black as an ace of spades. His bald head resembled a milk dud and his beady eyes added to his intimidating look. At the age of 36, he still had not grown a strand of facial hair which made his face look smooth as a baby's ass. Very seldom did he smile, but when he did his pearly white teeth was enough to light up a room. In spite of being an oversized and obese charcoal black man, he had a certain charisma and teddy bear swagger about himself that allowed him to charm his way into the likes of many individuals. He also had a ruthless demeanor and a body count that helped him excel into the circle of the drug cartels and gain fear and respect from the streets.

Big Black had worked his way up as being one of

the number one cocaine distributers in Houston, TX under the lead of Alejandro Guzman aka "Shorty" who was a boss for the Sinaloa Cartel. Big Black was Shorty's number one man. Whenever a shipment of kilos came into Houston they would first go to Shorty and Shorty would drop them off on Big Black.

Little did Shorty know, Big Black would re-rock the kilos and place his own stamp on them which enabled him to become a self-made millionaire in the drug game and eventually even have more money than his connect. The Bricks he was supplied with were so pure that the potency of the product was barely compromised enough for his clientele in the streets to ever notice they were recompressed. Even though Big Black had a million dollar home, a fleet of foreign cars, and hundreds of thousands of dollars' worth of jewelry, he made it a point to never shine or be flamboyant around Shorty or other cartel members.

He would usually wear a t-shirt, jeans, boots and drove around in an old pickup truck in their presence. The only thing Big Black made sure to lay on thick in front of Shorty was his conversation for money and dream to be like Pablo Escobar. He also made sure to lay his murder game down proper on several occasions for different members of the cartel to witness. They knew he was about his business and was more than capable to handle the streets and whatever came with them. Big Black had the dope game in the palm of his hands, but like most men he had a weakness. His weakness was pussy. He had a tricking habit bigger than the state of Texas. He had no kids, no family, no girlfriend, and his operation usually ran so smooth that he found nothing more interesting in his spare time to do except eat the finest foods and buy pussy. He didn't just like any pussy. He had a fetish for Latina pussy.

Big Black stood in the whore house on the southwest side of Houston with his pants down to his ankles as he pounded a big jiggly booty Latina from the back. He was a regular at the whore house and had fucked every Mexican whore there already at least 10 times each. All of the whores would only allow him to hit them from the back due to his giant physique and oversized belly, but that was also how he preferred it. Big Black thought he was hung like a horse from the way the whores would perform during sex, but in reality, his dick looked like a burnt, uncircumcised Vienna sausage.

"Ohh yes Papi! screamed the whore. Big Black was sweating like a pig and smelling like a mixture of Gucci Guilty cologne, Cheetos, and dog shit as he pounded away. He felt the pressure building up in his manhood and made a face looking like the man in the movie Green Mile when he was about to be executed and pulled off his condom and nutted on the prostitute's back. The girl was so relieved when their session was over that she ran out of the room forgetting her shirt leaving Big Black alone in his thoughts as his cell phone began to ring. He looked at the caller I.D. and saw that it was Alejandro "Shorty" Guzman.

"Yo, Wussup Boss?" He answered in his deep baritone Barry White voice.

Como estas mi amigo? I need you to stop by mi casa ASAP so we can talk. I have good news for you mi amigo."

"No problemo Boss. Say no more. I'll be there in a little while."

Big Black left the whore house leaving behind a generous tip and headed I-10 west to Katy, TX to meet Shorty at his home anxious to see what the unexpected call was for. When he pulled up to the residence, he had to press a button and announce his identity and presence on an intercom at the gate before he was granted access on the property. The gate was then opened by Shorty's gunmen who held assault rifles and identified him before allowing him to enter the 8-million-dollar estate. A long driveway led up to the massive home where a pond was at the edge of the front yard and semi-circle driveway. Inside of the pond was a spinning, electric sculpted statue of the globe that Shorty adopted from the movie Scarface that read "The World Is Mine." The house looked like a replica of the White House from the outside and goons were suited with guns at every 50 meters of the residence. When Big Black rang the doorbell, the first person he saw was Shorty's beautiful wife Esmerelda who welcomed him into the home.

"Hola Black! How are you? Come in. Shorty is expecting you!" "Que pasa Esmerelda? How are you?"
"I'm fine. I was just in the cocina making some homemade salsa. Do you want something to drink?"
"Si. I'll take a Sprite."

Big Black followed Esmerelda into the kitchen as he sat down at the kitchen table and stared at Esmerelda's flawless body. Esmerelda was beauty at it's finest. Her body was shaped like a coke bottle and her ass was loose and jiggly just how Big Black liked. Her face was pretty as a model and her big brown eyes were hypnotizing to look in. Her shoulder length silky black hair bounced with every step she took matching the rhythm of her ass cheeks as she moved throughout the kitchen wearing some black spandex tights and a pink wife beater that she had tied in a knot at the back exposing her flawless flat stomach.

Just as Big Black felt his erection growing in his

pants, Shorty walked in the kitchen wearing his boxer shorts with his eyes bucked wide open with an obvious amount of white powder around his nostrils. Shorty was amped up moving 100 miles per hour.

"Big Black! Que paso mi amigo! Mi hermano! El hambre dinero! Wussup!!" "What's up Shorty?" said Big Black as he stood and extended his hand to shake. "You know me boss. I've just been making this money trying to be like Escobar and looking for some big booty Latinas."

"Big Black. You black men really do like fat asses don't you? I think a fat ass on a woman means that she needs to lose weight!"

"You just have to know what to do with that ass Boss."

"Whatever my friend. I didn't call you here to talk about ass. I want to talk money. I have 100 kilos coming tomorrow and I need them all gone. How many can you get?"

"That depends on your price Boss."

"How about 18 a piece?"

"Boss man if you let me get them for 17 a piece, I'll buy all of them upfront." "OK Big Black. You got it primo. I'll even give you fifty more on consignment as a bonus. Now excuse me. I have to get ready for a fiesta tonight," he said sniffling and clapping his hands. "Make sure you give Big Black some of that salsa to take home Esmerelda."

Shorty grabbed his wife and kissed her as he skipped out of the kitchen with his fat stomach shaking and hanging over his boxer shorts. He looked like a short Mexican Danny Davito with a mustache high off cocaine with a bunch of money. Esmerelda looked to make sure Shorty was out of earshot as she began talking.

"You know what Big Black? You're right. Some men don't know what to do with an ass like this," she said smacking her ass.

She stepped to the table placing a Tupperware of salsa in front of Big Black and handed him a Sprite. Big Black seized the moment of Esmerelda putting her camel toe so close to his face by aggressively grabbing her around the waist and smelled her crotch area closing his eyes and taking in a deep breath. "What do you think you're doing?" she asked. Big Black turned her around and before she could say anything else to protest, he pulled down her black tights from the back and started to bravely lick the crack of her ass.

Esmerelda consented to the sneaky act by bending over and slightly arching her asshole on his tongue as he worked his magic while Shorty was right upstairs taking a shower. Unfortunately, for the two sneaky traitors, Esmerelda's little sister Maria walked around the corner and witnessed what her sister was doing behind her brother-n-law's back. She peeked into the kitchen and couldn't believe her eyes. Although Esmerelda didn't know she was being watched, she quickly came to her senses and pulled up her tights stepping away from Big Black's tongue.

"You're crazy! You know we shouldn't do this. Shorty would kill us!" "You're right Esmerelda. I'm sorry. I don't know what I was thinking." "It's ok. Just give me your cell phone number."

"I can't. Shorty knows my number. It wouldn't be good if you were caught with it."

"Give me one he doesn't have. He's going to the Valley soon. I will call you when he leaves."

Big Black quickly wrote his number to one of his burner phones down on a kitchen napkin and handed it to Esmerelda before leaving.

CHAPTER 8

Meanwhile, on the other side of the city, Anna had been web surfing and prospecting the most beautiful prostitutes she could find between the ages of 18 and 25. Not counting her master bedroom, she had four extra bedrooms she planned to fill with 2 girls each that would give her a total of 8 working girls under one roof. She figured if she could handle 8 girls properly at one time, then she could expand her operation in a year or two and buy a mansion tripling her stable. Although she wanted to make that power move now, she knew the importance of the cliche' "you have to crawl before you walk."

All week long she interviewed different girls around the city to see if they met the standards, she required to be a working girl at "Anna's Revival". She wanted nothing but the best. Every girl had to be physically flawless, drug free, clean, single and extremely pretty to even be considered. So far, her recruitment process was going perfectly. Her stable was almost complete.

She had 2 sexy white girls named Kelly and Jennifer, 2 beautiful big booty black girls named Sugar and Kandi, 2 of the baddest Asians in town by the name of Amy and Kim and 1 smoking hot Latina name Martha. Every one of the girls had to bring Anna a thousand dollars up front and eat her pussy before being welcomed into the house. She made sure she established the perimeters of who was boss from the beginning. The only fault in her plan was that she needed one more Latina to complete her stable. She was beginning to get frustrated in her search until finally she came across a gorgeous 23 year old Hispanic beauty soliciting on Backpage in Katy, TX with perfect perky titties and an ass that would make Jennifer Lopez jealous.

Anna gave the girl a call and set up a meeting to discuss business at a local Chili's near the girl's residence. For some reason, the girl was adamant about meeting her there insisting that Anna could not come to her residence.

Anna assumed the girl who introduced herself as Maria was staying with family and sneaking around to be a hoe which would make taking her away from home an easy task. When Anna spotted Maria at the

Chili's, she was pleased to see that she was even prettier in person. Maria had everything that it took to be eye candy on any TV station in the country of Mexico. Her look was exotic, and her body was everything that a man craved for.

Even as beautiful as Maria was, she was still star struck and felt intimidated in the presence of the aggressive and gorgeous Ms. Anna Davis. The two women sat down over lunch as they made their introductions and talked business.

"So... how long have you been on Backpage?" asked Anna "For about a week or so," Maria replied slightly embarrassed. "I see that you list your services for only $150 dollars an hour. Do you realize how much risk you are taking and the amount of danger you're putting yourself in for that amount of money?"

"Excuse me bitch!" Maria snapped with an attitude. "I thought you wanted to meet me here to discuss business. If you just want to judge me then maybe I shouldn't have met you here. You don't know anything about what I do and what kind of situation I've faced or capable of facing. You're just a pretty white lady without a clue."

Anna stared intensely into Maria's eyes trying to read her and bust into a wicked, uncontrollable laugh.

"Do you find something funny?" Maria asked "Yes, I do darling. You remind me of myself when I first got into the business. I love your attitude sweetie. You're going to need to use that against these tricks in this business. But for the record, I'm not a trick and I'm not the one to fuck with. Comprende?"

Anna pulled back her bleach blonde hair and showed Maria the scar embedded in her head from the bullet wound.

"Do you see that chica? That's from being shot in the head because I was once stupid like you. I've been selling 3-way love since you were probably playing hopscotch and Barbie dolls. Do you know what 3-way love is? It's head, pussy and ass and I have the best on the market. Don't ever underestimate me!"

"So what do you want?" asked Maria as she changed her tone of voice already feeling like Anna's little bitch.

"I have a proposition for you. I hate to see pretty girls like you undermining their talents on cheap sites like Backpage. Because I can relate to you, I don't want you to have to go through what I did and possibly get shot in the head or risk dying at the hands of some maniac out there. That's why I established my brothel that can provide protection for you and put you in a comfortable environment that will allow you to exert your talents. My list of clients is as long as the Nile River and I will ensure that you get $100 dollars an hour for your services along with the protection and client list I can provide for you. There are other girls working under MY roof just like you, and you will be part of our family. So what do you say?"

Maria thought about her options. She had nothing to lose and the sound of Anna's proposition sounded exciting and very rewarding considering she had only turned 2 tricks on her own that were both weird and dangerous experiences. She also wanted to feel like she was a part of something. Especially since she didn't feel like she was part of her current family much anyway. No one at home really paid her much attention and her constant need to be fucked and her desire to make money independently is what made her want to prostitute.

"What do I have to do to start?"

"You can start as soon as you give me a rack. That's the first requirement for all of my girls to cover first month's rent, utilities and food."

Maria reached in her pocket and handed Anna a thousand dollars. "Now what?"

"Now you come with me," Anna winked grabbing her hand leading her out. "I want you to taste Mama pootn tang pie. Welcome to Anna's Revival baby."

CHAPTER 9

Big Black sat in one of his apartments that he had ducked off on Rodgerdale Dr. and the Beltway recompressing his bricks with one of his henchmen from El Salvador. Even though he was connected with the Sinaloa Cartel as his supplier, he had personally selected a young group of MS-13 members to be his henchmen in the streets. All of his goons were from El Salvador and ruthless youngsters between the ages of 13 and 24. Big Black selected the young group after becoming familiar with one of them during a period he was tricking with the teenager's mother in a whore house. He became good friends with the whore and took her son in as his protege and recruited his neighborhood peers who were all broke to be his team of goons around Houston.

Big Black would pay people he knew with no criminal record to attend gun shows and buy him weapons. His favorite firearm was the AR-15 and he made sure to keep one in close proximity at all times. Big Black had stashed 100 bricks away at another one of his spots and was turning the 50 that he got on consignment now into 62 by cutting them with baking soda and getting an extra 9 ounces off each brick. After he was done cutting 50 bricks, he would ultimately have an extra 12 bricks for free. Shorty was charging him $17,000 apiece and he was selling them for $28,000 a piece which meant the 12 extra bricks would be an extra free $336,000 dollars. Big Black was licking his lips jamming his Kevin Gates c.d as he thought about all the pussy he would be buying over the next couple of months from his new shipment of blow.

Each brick he opened out the shipment from Shorty was Grade-A fish scale. Everyone was 98% pure before he put his cut on it. The bricks were official. Each one came wrapped in black electric tape around red radiator fluid in saran wrap and newspaper dressing with a baseball card of a deceased Columbian president in the middle. Big Black had a compressing machine that would leave an H-town stamp on the bricks to put his personal imprint and represent his work for out of towners.

His operation was simple. He would front a quarter of the bricks to his out of town connect Junior in Shreveport, LA. and another quarter of the supply to his out of town connect Worm in New Orleans, LA. The other half he distributed in Houston flooding the streets of 5th Ward, South Park and all of the Southwest side. Big Black had his henchmen load up his Tahoe with 15 bricks while he followed behind him headed to meet his man Junior from Shreveport at a nearby 24-Hour Fitness Gym on Westheimer.

The henchmen was driving the work in front of Big Black while he also made sure that another one of his goons followed behind him with an AR-15.

On the way to the 24-Hour Fitness Big Black noticed a house off of Westheimer with a wooden sign hanging by the door with flashing lights that read "Anna's Revival". To the normal law-abiding citizen, it wouldn't have come off as intriguing or raised antennas, but Big Black wasn't a law-abiding citizen. He was a drug dealer and a major trick all too familiar with what a whore house looked like. On that side of town brothels weren't uncommon and he knew it had to be a new one because he was familiar with all the old ones. He made a mental note to pay the house a visit the first chance he got.

CHAPTER 10

It didn't take long for Anna's brothel to start booming with business. She got in touch with all of her old clients and invited them to her house and turned them on to the new diverse fresh litter of pussy she harnessed. Needless to say, they were all pleased with her fine establishment and left with a happy ending on every visit that kept them coming back for more. Word of mouth spread quickly through the streets amongst tricks that "Anna's Revival" was the hottest new brothel in the city of Houston.

The house had a long driveway that led to the back of the house where Anna had the big backyard paved with concrete for clients to discreetly park behind the house. She had burglar bars and alarm system installed for her and the girl's safety. She also retired her pink handled .25 caliber for a pearl handled .9mm Glock that she kept tucked on her loaded at all times.

When a trick would enter the front door, he would be expected to hand over $300 dollars directly to Anna in exchange for a massage. Once Anna received the money, she would ring a bell and the girls would come from the back and line up in the living room wearing only a bra and a thong. The trick would then point to the woman of his choice and be led to the restroom where the girl would shower him and then lead him to her room where she'd service him with mind blowing safe sex. On a good night, the brothel would turn 8 tricks in an hour. Sometimes a trick would have to wait for a few short minutes in the living room because the rooms would be full. However, most times the tricks never spent the full hour in the room that they paid for and everything worked out perfectly. After 15 minutes, they usually would cum and leave happy. The brothel ran 24 hours a day 7 days a week and gave Anna's girls only enough time to take cat naps.

On the nights when the brothel turned 8 tricks an hour at $300 an hour for 24 hours, it was an easy $57,600 for one day. Anna told the girls she would put up their $100 dollars an hour and she kept her word depositing all of it in a separate safe for each girl.

In 90 days Anna had accumulated $325,000 dollars of her own money and saved at least $125,000 for each one of her girls Although they never saw the money, they knew it was there because she would occasionally count it out in front of them to keep them focused. She usually kept them happy by treating them to the finest restaurants and taking them to the spa, the beautician, Message Envy and getting them pedicures and manicures when business was slow. Finally, one day she decided to keep the girls broke by treating them to something more expensive and fancier with their savings. Anna rented a limo and loaded the girls up and took them to the tattoo shop.

She officially gave her girls a name in her stable and labeled them as "The Sophisticats". Anna felt that the name Sophisticat was appealing to her girls considering the way she had trained them to be sophisticated in the way they sold their cat. Each girl got a tattoo on their right ass cheek of a black panther with capital italic letters above the panther that read "Sophisticat".

After leaving the tattoo shop, she took them to Mike Smith Auto Plaza and purchased each one of her hoes brand new convertible Camaros. The next day she had the cars delivered to a nearby paint and body shop and painted each car hot pink. She went a step further and bought 20-inch lime green Asanti rims for each car and had Cat on all the license plates. Each license plate was printed with Cat #1, Cat #2 and so on and so on according to the order in which they were recruited. Maria was Cat #8 since she had been recruited last and Jennifer happened to be Cat #1.

The girls were ecstatic. Especially Maria. She seemed to be living her dream. They had to park the cars in the back of the brothel and get back to work because Anna let it be known that she had spent all of their money and she was tough on them about recouping it all back. The clientele Anna received at her new whore house was much more diverse than the clients she was used to servicing over the internet. Her new way of income was not only different, but also more dangerous. Anna took every precaution imaginable to protect herself and the girls, but the danger of the business always was prevalent.

Men of all races, creeds, colors, religions, and professions were visiting the brothel. Whenever you have women, sex and money there will also always be another demon lurking around called drugs. Anna noticed that many of the clients that sometimes came in also wanted drugs specifically cocaine. Other clients were obvious drug dealers who came in smelling like marijuana. Where some people might have saw this as a problem, Anna saw it as an opportunity. She instinctively thought about how she could also make money in the drug business and suddenly realized she needed a drug connect, so she could innovate a new income of wealth into her safe deposit box.

CHAPTER 11

The date was Valentine's Day, February 14th and also All-Star Weekend in Houston, Tx. Anna's brothel had been going full fledge for the last past 5 months. By Anna being a veteran hoe, she knew that everybody who was somebody would be in the city tonight and throughout the weekend. She also knew that her regular tricks would be coming through, but the real big money would be under the city lights in the circles of the rich and famous. She summoned all of the girls into the living room and made an OG call that would turn out to be their Valentine's Day gift.

"Listen up bitches. We've been working really hard for the last few months and I want ya'll to know that I'm proud of each and every one of you. Tonight, is Valentines night and the only love I have is for my money and the bitches working in my house. We are a family. I'm closing the brothel for tonight and taking all of you out for Valentine's tonight."

"Yayyy!" The girls clapped.

"Wait a minute! Before ya'll bitches get too excited. I want ya'll to remember something. It's also All-Star Weekend and there will be money all around the city so stay focus. Remember who you are. Sophisticats! And remember what you do. Remember we are family and remember who mama is. Now I want each one of you to find your hottest outfit because tonight is the night we turn up!"

Anna's girls were overwhelmed with excitement as they began to leap for joy and ran to their rooms to play dress up and decide what they would wear for the night. Maria stayed behind in the living room looking slightly irritated.

"Is there a problem Maria?" asked Anna

"No. I'm glad we're going out. It's just that I have a bad ass pair of Red Bottom shoes I wanna wear, but they're not here.

"Where are they?"

"They're at my sister and brother-n-law house in Katy."

"Well I suggest you hurry up and go get them before it's too late. I'll grab your car keys."

Anna went to the master bedroom to retrieve Maria's car keys. When she handed them to Maria, she lit up like a kid at Christmas time. "Oooh thanks Anna! I'll be right back!"

Maria raced to her sister's estate that she shared

with Shorty as she jammed to 97.9 The Box on the radio station singing along word for word to Beyoncé's latest single while hoping she wouldn't run into anybody while she was there. She had only been back and forth to the house in the last 5 months probably only once a month and hated explaining her whereabouts to her older sister and Shorty.

When she got to the estate, she asked one of the gunmen if they seen Shorty and they told her he was in the Valley and her sister Esmerelda had just left headed to the store. She quickly ran upstairs to get her shoes and left out quick as she could.

While driving down Fry Rd. in Katy, Maria spotted her sister Esmerelda in her 745 BMW a few cars ahead of her stopped at a traffic light. Surprisingly instead of Esmerelda going to a store, Maria noticed her turn into a cheap hotel. Maria bust a U-turn and slowly entered the hotel parking lot as she saw her sister walking into a hotel room with the same big black guy who she witnessed licking her sister's ass a few months back.

Maria had later found out that the man known as Big Black worked for Shorty. She knew her sister was playing a dangerous game. She couldn't resist parking and going peek through the window to confirm her suspicions. What she saw through the window blew her mind. Esmerelda was completely naked rubbing KY Jelly in her anus as she let Big Black fuck her in the ass without a condom. Maria walked away from the window disgusted by the sight and headed back to Anna's.

CHAPTER 12

The city of Houston was lit! Everyone from all parts of the country had traveled to the 4th largest city in America to be present for All Star Weekend and party with the stars. The Galleria was packed with celebrities partaking in recreational shopping and being bombarded by Houstonians to take selfies for their social media. Every street seemed to be packed with traffic as people traveled to some sort of party or event for the night.

Anna had purchased a V.I.P section for her and her 8 hoes at the Toyota Center where Jeezy and Drake were scheduled to perform. Each girl was uniquely beautiful in her own way and the crowd of women had everybody's attention the moment they stepped in the building. After the concert, Anna had her girls follow her to Club Dreams while she drove her white on white droptop Aston Martin V12 Vantage S Roadster and the Sophisticats trailed behind in a single file line in their hot pink droptop Camaro's with lime green 20 inch Asantis.

Out of all the celebrities who were at the strip club, nobody was a sight to see like Anna and the Sophisticats as they lined up with their fleet of cars in valet parking. When they stepped out of their vehicles all eyes were on them. They were granted immediate access into the club as Anna gave the bouncer a cool thousand-dollar tip to jump the line. Anna immediately bought the last V.I.P section in the club and bought enough bottles of Ciroc to keep their table sparkling all night long. The girls were having a blast as they drank under Anna's focused supervision and mingled with the biggest ballers all night long. No man who was broke dared to step up to the girls as they accepted money all night long from different men and made it rain on the strippers and occasionally got lap dances just for the fun of it.

Usually Big Black would never step foot in a strip club, but on this particular night he made an exception and was watching Anna and her entourage of hoes from a distance with one of his henchmen named Mario.

"Yo, Mario! Who the fuck is them fine ass bitches over there splurging like that!" he yelled over the music as the D.J was playing "Throw Some Commas!" by Future.

"I don't know Boss! I never saw them before, but they sure making it rain!"

"Well go over there and find out!" Big Black barked.

Mario eased his way into the section of the Sophisticats and started to mingle with Anna. Anna was experienced enough to know Mario was a flunky and someone had sent him, so she kept the conversation short and sweet.

She also made sure to tell him that she was about to make it rain on the strip hoes all night with her dope money. Mario fell for the bait and went back to give Big Black the little info he could gather up.

"Yo Boss! I still don't know who those hoes are, but that white girl looks like she the leader of the pack and her name Anna, and she slipped up and said she sell dope!"

"What? A white girl selling weight in my city and I don't know her? Tell that bitch to come here! Let her know Big Black need to holla at her!"

Mario played his flunkie position well as he went back and told Anna that Big Black wanted to speak with her and pointed in his direction. Anna followed Mario and approached Big Black grilling him not at all intimidated by his size.

"Wussup my nigga?" said Anna

"Nigga? Bitch who you calling a nigga?"

"Nigga who you calling a bitch?"

"Do you know who the fuck I am?" asked Big Black

"Do you know who the fuck I am?" asked Anna

"Naw, but what's this I hear about you moving weight in my city? What you know about that real white girl?"

"Your city? Hmmm. I know what I know, and I know if you can't hook me up then we don't have shit to talk about."

"That's where you wrong. I can hook you up with whatever you want. 28 thee a key. I'm the black Pablo Escobar around this bitch. You better ask somebody about me," Big Black boasted.

Anna really didn't know anything about cocaine how she was portraying, but she did know how to put on her poker face. She also knew how to talk slick and knew she had an extra $100 thousand dollars to play with.

"28? How about 25 and I'll spend a 100k with you Big Daddy?"

When Anna called Big Black Big Daddy and fed his ego, she had him. He was all for it.

"Aight snow bunny. We'll link up. Get my number from my man Mario right here."

"O.K. Big Daddy," Anna reiterated.

"And wussup with your big booty Latina homegirl down there?" Big Black asked while licking his lips and pointing at Maria.

"Oh, that's Maria. She'll go, but you can't have champagne taste and beer money to holla at one of my girls."

Big Black looked at Anna like she was stupid.

"Don't insult me snow bunny. Make it happen," he said with an arrogant attitude. "We'll see," said Anna as she handed Big Black a business card. Big Black looked at the card and read the phone number under the title "Anna's Revival" and smiled at Anna as she walked back to her section with her girls.

During the interim of All-Star Weekend, Anna met four big time drug dealers who were in the cocaine business. She met one through her black bitch Kandi who was a young black guy and a Blood in L.A, she met one who was an older hustler from Baltimore in the strip club, she met another one at an afterparty who was a white guy who managed rappers in Detroit and she met one at her brothel who was a Mexican who hustled on the Northside of Houston in Greens point. Her next objective was to hook up with Big Black and get some bricks so she could be their supplier.

CHAPTER 13

Anna called Big Black the following Monday and arranged a meeting with him. She was instructed to go to an address in South Park off of M.L.K Blvd. When Anna pulled up to the residence, she could tell that it was an obvious trap house. The house looked rundown from the outside and sat behind a five-foot hurricane gate with multiple cars in the driveway with pit bulls chained in the corner of the front yard and No Trespassing signs hanging on the gate. A few young Hispanics and young black guys stood outside with their pants sagging drinking out of big white Styrofoam cups and traffic was pulling up and away from the house like a drive-thru CVS pharmacy. Anna pulled out her cell phone and called Big Black to let him know she was there.

"Hello," he answered.

"Hey. I'm here outside at that address you gave me."

"Ok stay right there. Don't get out the car until I

pull up. I'll be there in a minute."

Anna sat in the car peeping her surroundings and casing the trap-house until Big Black pulled up behind her and signaled for her to get out the car. Anna got out holding her oversized Prada bag with her Glock 9 tucked in the front of her jeans with her shirt hanging loosely over her waist. If an unknown white lady had showed up to that trap-house alone it would've been trouble. Luckily for Anna she was with Big Black so everyone there knew it had to be official business. Big Black led Anna to the kitchen where he sat down at the head of the kitchen table looking like a grizzly bear twirling his thumbs and grilling Anna with his beady eyes. Anna sat down across from him at the other end of the table grilling him back.

"What you got for me snow bunny?" he asked.
"What you got for me?" she responded.

Big Black looked at his flunkie Mario and gave him a nod. Mario went to the back and came back into the kitchen with four bricks of cocaine and a digital scale. He placed the bricks in front of Anna and placed each brick separately on the scale showing that each one was weighing a thousand grams. Anna emptied her Prada bag and let the $100,000 dollars she had fall on the kitchen table. The money was in ten 10 thousand-dollar stacks with the bank bands wrapped around them. Mario reached in the kitchen cabinet and pulled out a money machine and immediately began running the money through the machine while Anna and Big Black made small talk.

"Don't you wanna test that bitch?" Big Black asked.

Anna really didn't like to snort coke because it seemed like it made her overly aggressive and in the past when she did it, Lil Riley would always end up kicking her ass by the end of the night. However, she knew that Big Black was testing her to make sure she wasn't a cop. She took a line of dust off the middle of one of the bricks with her car keys and tilted her head back and sniffed some of the product in each one of her nostrils. The euphoria from the narcotic hit her seconds later as she immediately started to feel like Superwoman and contemplated on beating Big Black ass and robbing his trap-house.

"I'm gonna need more of this stuff. This not shit. This chump change for me," said Anna.
"Oh really? Don't worry. It's plenty more where that came from." "Good because I'll have this gone in no time."
"How long you been running that new house off of Westheimer?" asked Big Black "What difference do it make? When are you going to pay us a visit?"

"Is that fine Latina bitch who was at Club Dreams with you staying there?"

"I guess you'll have to stop by and find out."

"I guess I will. How we looking over there, Mario?"

"It's all there, Boss," Mario replied.

"Good. Air seal that shit for Ms. Anna so she can be on her way."

Mario air sealed the bricks for Anna in freezer bags as she put them in her Prada bag and safely drove from South Park back to her house in the Westchase District blending in with 5 o'clock traffic. Luckily for Anna, her out of town buyers from L.A., Detroit and Baltimore had extended their visits and were still in Houston waiting for the product that Anna said she could provide at a better price than what they were getting.

She met with them and sold them each a kilo for 30 thousand. She then met her buyer on the North side and sold him a kilo for 28 thousand. From 5pm to 10pm Anna made an easy 18-thousand-dollar profit on her first day in the cocaine business. She made sure to make arrangements with her out of town suppliers on how she would soon be delivering more weight into their cities and not be dealing with anything less than 10 keys at a time. By midnight she was at home and Big Black was ringing the doorbell at "Anna's Revival."

CHAPTER 14

Anna opened the door and welcomed Big Black in as she crossed her arms and stood in front of him staring up at his gigantic frame. It was nights like this that Anna was glad she wasn't selling pussy anymore. Although if the price was right, she would still turn a trick, but she would prefer to fuck someone much smaller and more attractive than Big Black. Lately Anna had been getting her orgasms off from her "B.O.B" (Battery Operated Boyfriend) and getting her pussy ate by her hoes. She had sold pussy for so long that all dick felt the same and she never felt affection for anyone except for her deceased pimp Lil Riley, so she just preferred to be celibate nowadays.

"Welcome to Anna's Revival! I'm so glad you finally decided to visit. Our massages are $300 dollars and they ALWAYS come with a happy ending."

Big Black smiled exposing his pearly white teeth and peeled Anna off $300 bucks. In the streets he was a ruthless drug boss, but when he got in a whore house, he seemed to melt into a big charming teddy bear.

Anna put the money in her bra and rang a bell on the wall. Within seconds, all eight of her hoes lined up in the living room looking gorgeous as ever and close to naked. Big Black's eyes passed up all the girls and landed straight on Maria as he pointed. Maria instantly recognized Big Black and was slightly disappointed she was picked this time. However, Big Black was happier than a punk in a dick factory completely unaware that Maria was Shorty's sister-n-law. Maria led Big Black to the back for a quick shower and to perform 20 minutes of sexual gratification that seemed to be the longest 20 minutes of her life.

After Big Black came from the back of the house smiling like a big goofy bear, Anna was sitting in the living room waiting for him to discuss business. It was obvious from the spark in Big Black's eyes that Maria did a splendid job and Anna knew she had discovered his weakness.

How'd you like my girl?" Anna asked.

"I like her! I love a Latina with a big jiggly booty. You should get more girls like her."

"I plan on it. Right now, I need more of those blocks. I'm done with the four I bought earlier today. I need 40."

"Whoa! You already tryna do it like that Snowbunny? At 25 a piece that's gonna cost you a ticket. You got a mill to play with?"

"Don't try to count my pockets. I said I want the shit. Can you get it or not? If not, I'll find someone who can."

"Ok cool. I can get it. Just make sure your bread right."

"My bread just like my hoes pussy. It's on point every time. You just Make sure you bring that shit to my doorstep and don't ever have me meet you in no rundown trap-house in South Park again. And make sure it's the same shit. I'm not just some dumb ass white bitch, nigga."

"Ok. Whatever. You got that Snowbunny."

"And Big Black...one more thing."

"Wussup?"

"Stop calling me Snowbunny. My name is Ms. Anna Davis. Remember the name and respect the game. Now if you will...please excuse yourself from my brothel. Your one hour that you payed for has expired."

Big Black proceeded to exit the house with a new level of respect for Anna. He was not only impressed by Maria, but he was also impressed by Anna and glad that he made the connection. With Anna buying that many bricks at one time he would be a step closer to his Escobar dream and also would have more access to new pussy through Anna's Revival.

CHAPTER 15

Three months passed by and Anna was moving more dope than the law allow and still running a successful whore house at the same time. Between her four buyers she was easily selling 40 kilos a week with each one of her buyers buying 10 keys a week except for her out of town buyer in Baltimore who was only able to buy five. Anna usually would front him the other five on consignment and he'd pay her later.

She contacted an old wealthy trick of hers who owned a private jet and sold him on the idea to give her and her girls free trips every week in exchange for accommodating dates and free top of the line pussy whenever he wanted. The old wealthy white man was a magnate in the oil industry and more than obliged to help assist Anna in safely transporting her drugs where they needed to be for the sake of keeping eye candy on his shoulders in the presence of his business colleagues. Not including the profits from the brothel, Anna was profiting $180 thousand dollars a week from drug sells that equaled up to $720,000 dollars a month of extra income. She had more money now than she knew what to do with. Her only plan was to buy a mansion and get more hoes to work for her. While Big Black was striving to be the black Pablo Escobar, Anna was also striving to be the white Griselda Blanca.

Anna couldn't understand how all of her buyers seemed to be coming up except for the guy in Baltimore who she was always helping to get ahead. She decided to send her black hoes Sugar and Kandi to Baltimore to do some research on him. Sugar and Kandi worked in a strip club while in Baltimore and found out that the guy had an expensive tricking habit on strippers. He also was a heroin dealer and a heroin junkie at the same time which explained his setbacks in his cocaine business with Anna. One day when Anna was ready to collect and re-distribute, she kept calling his phone and didn't get an answer. Another week went by and his number was disconnected.

Without any hesitation, Anna flew to Baltimore with her two Asian hoes Amy and Kim and devised a murderous plot without pondering the consequences. Anna found out the dry cleaners where the guy brought his clothes and she paid the owner a hefty amount to let her, Amy and Kim work there for a few days without anything in return except to make sure that no cameras were working. Just like clockwork, the guy came in to drop off his clothes. Kim and Amy were working in the front while Annna sat in the back playing Pokeman on her cell phone. When Kim went to the back to advise Anna the man she was waiting for was there, Amy pretended to print out his ticket for his clothes. Anna came from the back with a silencer attached to her Clock 9 and released two shots in the guy face before he knew what happened. He never saw it coming. Anna was courteous enough to dump his body in the dumpster with the help of her girls to avoid bringing heat on the cleaners. After her work was done, they flew back to Texas like nothing happened.

The more work Anna bought from Big Black, the more Big Black bought from Shorty and the more work Shorty moved, the more the Sinaloa Cartel ate. Everyone was happy. Especially Big Black. He seemed to be the luckiest drug dealer alive. He was still fucking the plugs wife Esmerelda on a regular basis and now he was fucking Maria at least twice a week too.

Anna noticed the frequent visits to her house from Big Black and could tell that Maria had him hooked.

One day she finally brought it up to Maria while they were eating breakfast together at a nearby IHOP.

"What's up with you and Big Black? I see he visits a lot and only request for you."

"Nothing is up. I just think he has a thing for Latinas."

"Well you must have him pussy whipped chica because he can't stay away from you."

"He doesn't want me. He wants my sister Esmerelda."

"Your sister? What makes you say that?"

"It's true. He doesn't know who I am, but I recognize him. He buys drugs from my brother-n-law Shorty and I caught him and my sister fucking before. I just never told anyone because Shorty would kill her if he found out. He's a member of the cartel and where we are from in Mexico men are known to behead their wives when they cheat on a cartel boss like Shorty."

"Oh shit!" said Anna "It's such a small world. Just make sure you don't let him know and keep making your money off that motherfucker chica. Your secret is safe with me."

Little did Maria know, Anna had secret cameras installed in every room. She had seen Big Black sliding Maria extra money on every occasion he would visit. Maria was secretly stashing. The money was no big deal, but the principle of stashing money away from Anna in her house was unacceptable. That was the main reason Anna sparked up the conversation to see if Maria would mention it and come clean. However, now Anna had now dug up something more valuable. Now that Maria had given Anna this new pertinent information, she started to conjure a masterplan on how to kill two birds with one stone.

CHAPTER 16

A few weeks passed by and Anna was on Big Black's and Maria's trail watching closely to every step they made with the help of a private investigator. She kept Maria close and even let her take a few trips with her out of state when she was making drops and picking up money. Anna made sure to bring at least two of her hoes with her on every trip disguising them as getaways for the girls and of course she always had dates arranged for them to work as escorts. Maria had become a high commodity and was often requested by the hobbyist in every state.

It didn't take long for Anna and her private investigator to realize that Big Black kept goons riding in front and behind him during his daily operations. For a low level drug dealer or inexperienced cop to try and rob him, kill him or bust him would seem almost impossible, but because Big Black was so myopic with his tricking habits, Anna identified his weakness and his vulnerability.

He was so discreet with his affairs with Esmerelda that he never let anyone know of his whereabouts when they were together. Not even his goons. The private investigator was able to take pictures of Big Black and Esmerelda meeting at the motel on several occasions. Some of the pictures showed them kissing right outside of the motel door and other photographs were even able to catch them engaged in the act of sex through the motel window.

By following Maria, Anna was able to find out the estate where Alejandro "Shorty" Guzman and Esmerelda lived. She even had tabs placed on Shorty to get close to him. Unlike Big Black, Shorty's operation was much more sophisticated and even though he sniffed coke all day, he moved with the precision of a real boss and stayed protected with a small army. Breaking into Shorty's infrastructure began to seem impossible for Anna until her milestone came when her and her private investigator found a repetition in Shorty's schedule.

Shorty would go play golf at Bear Creek Country Club every Thursday at 2pm except for the days he was in the Valley. Anna now knew exactly when and where she could contact him when the time was right.

Anna also got bits and bits of information from Maria without allowing Maria to become suspicious of her plot. On this particular day Anna made small talk with Maria to fish for information.

"What's up chica? You never told me what did your sister and brother-n-law say about your new car."

"They didn't say much. They just asked where did I get it. I told them I bought it with my own money I saved up from working at my new job as a waitress."

"Do they ever say they miss you being at home?"

"Hell no. They could care less. They think I have my own apartment now. Shorty is in the Valley most of the time and my sister stays gone shopping and playing like a queen with his money."

"How often is Shorty in the Valley?" asked Anna.

"He goes at least twice a month. Sometimes three and he always stay gone three or four days at a time. I stopped by there yesterday when you let me off to get my nails done and my sister said he was there now."

"Well it's a good thing you have all the family you need here with us. Don't even worry about them chica. Mama Anna will always be here for you."

Without Maria having the slightest hint, Anna had just juiced her for the info she needed. She knew that Shorty was out of town and knew that Esmerelda and Big Black would be hooking up for one of their routine rendezvous in a matter of hours just like always.

CHAPTER 17

After three weeks of close surveillance on Big Black, Anna knew exactly what time to leave home and get on his trail. She hopped in her Jeep and brought her white hoe Jennifer to accompany her on her mission. Big Black had become so predictable over the last few weeks that it was ridiculous. Anna reckoned that he must've had a stroke of good luck and been blessed by the Game God to have made it so far up the ranks of the dope game.

Never in a million years could she have pictured her ex pimp Lil Riley being dumb as Big Black or figure him out.

Just as expected, Big Black and Esmerelda met at the same exact motel where they always met at the same exact time. Anna sat in her Jeep as she watched them enter into the motel room. She screwed a silencer onto her Clock 9 and put a stocking cap over her blonde hair and slid on a baseball cap. "This is too easy," she thought to herself. She reached in her hand rest and grabbed a hunting knife, a sharp knife used for cutting cheese and slipped on some latex gloves. Jennifer looked at Anna from the passenger seat like a loyal puppy and asked...

"What's the plan?"

"I want you to go knock on the door and raise hell asking for your husband to come out. When the door opens, step aside and come sit back in the Jeep. I'll take it from there."

Jennifer and Anna got out of the Jeep and approached the door as Jennifer started raising hell trying to beat the door down.

"Come out of there bitch! I know you're in there with my husband!" Yelled Jennifer. Big Black and Esmerelda were butt ass naked and Big Black had Esmerelda's knees to her chest with an inch of his tongue licking deep in her ass hole when they heard the irate woman outside who obviously had the wrong door.

Big Black jumped up and peeked out the peephole concluding that the woman had the wrong room. When he opened the door to avoid the disturbance and correct the lady, Anna came out of nowhere and kicked the door open with her pistol pointed dead in Big Black's face. Instead of reaching for Anna or a pistol, Big Black reached down trying to cover his little boy dick attached to his grown man body. When Big Black realized it was Anna holding him at gunpoint he felt like a complete debacle. Anna shot him in his knee and debilitated him instantly before he tried to make any hero moves. Esmerelda tried to scream but was silenced forever with a silent shot to her chest.

"Pheww!"

"Please Anna! Don't kill me!" pleaded Big Black "I'll give you whatever you want!"

Anna got a high off of seeing how even the biggest and baddest motherfucker bowed down and begged for their life when a gun was in their face and felt the burn of a bullet.

"Where the muthafuckin money and dope at, you big bitch ass nigga!"

"It's at my house Anna! I'll take you to it! Just please don't kill me!"

"What's your address? Where it's at? And don't lie!"

"25311 Boudreaux Estates! I swear! That's not a trap house Anna! That's where I stay for real, for real! All the dope and money under a secret compartment under my bedroom rug. Take all the dope and leave the money!" said Big Black covering his dick with one hand and holding his knee with the other.

"Muthafucka what! Take the dope and leave the money?"

"Pheww!" Anna shot Big Black in his other knee as he wailed and cried like a bitch.

"Owwww! Please don't kill me! Pleeaasse!" He cried.

Anna grabbed his pants and searched his wallet and found his license According to his driver's license and the looks in his eyes he was telling the truth. Anna aimed the gun between Big Black's eyes and sent him to his maker.

"Pheww!"

She then grabbed her hunting knife and chopped off Esmerelda's head and put it in a pillow case she then took the cheese knife and chopped off Big Black's dick and wrapped it nice and neat in a motel towel. Jennifer was still in the Jeep waiting for her when she left out the room and unaware of the contents that Anna threw on the backseat when they left the premises.

Anna dropped Jennifer home and went to Big Black's house. Just as he promised, there was more drugs and money in his secret spot than Anna had seen in her life. It took her a full hour to carry all the money and kilos out of his house and stuff it the best she could into her jeep. She transported everything back to her garage in her brothel and knew that she needed to buy a mansion as soon as possible. She was officially in a league of her own.

CHAPTER 18

When Shorty got back from the Valley, the first thing he received from one of his henchmen was the pictures taken by the private investigator of Big Black and Esmerelda that had mysteriously showed up on the front lawn. He was furious. He wanted them dead. Within minutes of receiving the photos, he was notified by the news on TV of the double homicide that occurred at the motel down the street from his residence.

The murders ironically sounded a lot like the victims could be Big Black and Esmerelda, but the police couldn't identify the body of the woman. Even Maria stopped by and told Shorty about her suspicions of the dead woman being Esmerelda. Shorty was in a menacing mood and a confused state of mind. All he could think about was how, who, and when? As he put the pieces of the puzzle together, he concluded that his wife was indeed fucking his number one man and now someone had possibly murdered them both. He couldn't help but wonder if that someone was going to try and kill him next. It was Thursday afternoon and he needed to retreat to the place where he could find refuge and could gather his thoughts until things made sense. He headed to the golf course at Bear Creek Country Club just like Anna knew he would.

When Shorty pulled up to the country club he was escorted out of Lexus SUV by his henchmen. Anna was parked a few spots away and got out of her Jeep wasting no time approaching Shorty with a pillowcase in one hand and a motel towel in the other. Before Anna could get within 10 feet of Shorty, his goons had their pistols drawn and ready to shoot Anna if she came any closer. Anna was wearing a black business suit made for a woman and was wearing dark Dolce and Gabbana sunshades, with some stockings and black pumps. She looked more like she had just left a funeral or like an employee from the D.A.s office than a prostitute or drug dealer.

"Excuse me Mr. Guzman. May I have a moment of your time please?"

"Who are you and how do you know my name? If this has anything to do with arresting me I have nothing to say to you and would like to call my lawyer." "Arrest you? Oh no Mr. Guzman. Please tell your men to lower their guns.

I'm not a cop and I definitely don't want to see you in jail Shorty."

Shorty signaled for his gunmen to lower their weapons.

"Well who the fuck are you!"

"Let's just say I'm a friend. I know about the pictures Shorty."

At the mention of the pictures Shorty now became extremely curious and wanted to hear what Anna had to say.

"Ok. Let me hear what you have to say."

Shorty and Anna sat at a bench in front of the country club while his goons stood a few feet away and allowed them a little privacy to talk. Anna was completely honest with Shorty. (Almost) She told him how Maria was working in her brothel and how Maria told her about Big Black fucking Esmerelda. She then went on to say how important she felt loyalty was and how she lost respect for Big Black and Esmerelda when she heard about their fling and felt they should die for betraying Shorty. She admitted to killing them both and saying that her only regret was that she no longer had a connect to get her drugs.

The whole time she talked she was secretly playing on Shorty's emotions to get what she really wanted all along. She left out the part about robbing Big Black. She left the part out about how she even knew where Shorty would be at that specific time and she left the part out that she really killed Big Black to get close to his supplier. Shorty was almost convinced, but he still had one question. "That's an impressive story Ms. Anna Davis. I just need to know something. How the fuck do I know you're not a federal agent and why would I trust you or anything that you just said?"

Anna unwrapped the motel towel and dropped Big Black's little black dick on the pavement for him to see.

"Do you see that? I chopped that un loyal Nigger's dick off for you Shorty. He had no business sleeping with your wife."

Anna handed Shorty the pillowcase with Esmerelda's head in it. "Take a look at that."

Shorty looked inside the pillowcase and saw Esmerelda's head with her eyes still wide open looking back at him. He quickly handed Anna the pillowcase back and started to puke on the pavement from the sight and smell of the head.

"You can trust me Shorty," said Anna. "I'm nothing like them. I'm as loyal as they come, and we can be allies and make a lot of money together. I will never betray you. I know what it feels like to be betrayed by someone you love. I did this for you because I will never let two unworthy muthafuckas like them get in the way of my money."

Shorty couldn't do anything from that moment but respect Anna's gangsta and hand her Big Black's seat at his table. She had earned the crown and accomplished what nobody else could do before her time.

"How much was Big Black giving you the keys for?"
"18 thousand a piece," lied Anna.
"I'll give them to you for 15," said Shorty.
"Good! Because I'll need 200 by this weekend. Here's my phone number."

Anna handed Shorty her phone number and just like that her mission was accomplished. She now had the keys to the city and was even able to get the work 2 thousand dollars cheaper than what Big Black was getting it for.

CHAPTER 19

Within a month Anna had closed on her dream home which of course was a mansion. Ironically, the cost of the mansion was paid for with Big Black's money and cost 6.8 million dollars. The property was a 30 plus acres, 10 thousand plus square foot custom designed home with 10 bedrooms, 12 bathrooms, 5 fireplaces, a gazebo, 3 Jacuzzis and a pool located in River Oaks. Interior features included a gourmet kitchen, an elevator, a wine cellar, a 1,600-square foot gym and a theater. Anna was living every drug dealer's dream. She was on top of her game and had money coming out the ass. Figuratively and literally speaking.

Most people would have chilled and lived comfortably with the millions of dollars she had, but not Anna. Anna just went harder with her hustle. She now established drug connections in Chicago, Atlanta, New York and New Orleans to add to the list of clientele she already had in L.A, Detroit and Houston. Every city that she went to she was able to give her buyers a cheap enough price to take over their city.

To avoid being tested, Anna always asked her buyers who were their competition and who did they have a problem with in their city. Before she left their city she would lure her prey in with one of the Sophisticats and chop their dick off, shoot them in the head and take a picture of the murder scene with her victim naked and his own dick stuck in his ass. She would then leave the picture with her buyer letting them know she handled their problem and warn them to never fuck over her. Her message was loud and clear.

Now that she had her mansion, she was able to send her original 8 Sophisticats to different cities and work as escorts. They were expected to make deposits automatically into Anna's business account every 3 days. By this time, they knew not to ever come up short on their quota or the punishment would be severe. With Anna's original 8 hoes on the road, she now had time to recruit more, but it required more foot work and prestige this time. Anna wanted nothing but the best living under her mansion.

She visited 5 countries and recruited 2 of the baddest hoes she could find in each country. She recruited 2 Brazilians, 2 Russians, 2 Germans, 2 Italians and 2 bad ass Puerta Ricans. All of them were the most exquisite site to see. Anna sped up the process to get them in America by showing them how to acquire working VISAS and applied them to work temporarily in America as maids at the address of her old brothel. However, once she got them to America, she had no intention on returning them back to their country when their working VISAS expired. If immigration ever went to their known address, they would find an empty house at the old brothel's address. Within 6 months Anna had 10 more Sophisticats with a black panther tattoo on their ass and an official Sophisticat stamp confirming their new family ties and acknowledging Anna as the mama cat and queen. The other Sophisticats were still paying automatic with no problems until one day...

CHAPTER 20

Maria was working out in Las Vegas in the casino posted at a bar at the MGM when she was approached by a handsome white man in a suit and tie. Although Maria wasn't a rookie, she still wasn't hip enough for the Las Vegas Prostitution Task Force that monitored the casinos. She bit the bait of an undercover agent and was arrested for prostitution and illegal possession of a firearm by a felon.

The prostitution charge wouldn't have been that bad alone, but because Maria had served 18 months in TDC before for theft a year before she met Anna, the felon in possession of a firearm charge was Federal. Once the Fedz stepped in and started talking football numbers to Maria unless she co-operated and gave up her pimp, she started singing like Kelly Clarkson. Maria called Anna and set up the play that would let her walk.

Anna was at home at the mansion lying by the pool in a lawn chair under the Texas sun drinking a

Mimosa while two of her bitches took turns eating her pussy when the phone rang...

"Unnn...Hell...Hello?"

"Hey mami. What's up?"

"Unn...Oooohh! What's up chica?" moaned Anna

"I'm out here in Vegas getting this money. You know how I do when you send me somewhere. I was just calling to let you know I'll be depositing that money to you later. You should come out here. I think you could get more girls."

"That sounds good chica. I'll see. Book mama a ticket and email me my boarding pass and itinerary. I'll see wussup. Unn! ! Gotta go. I'll mmm...talk to you later."

Anna hung up the phone and began to cum not knowing that the Feds were listening to her whole conversation. A week later she flew into Las Vegas and met Maria and a pretty brunette lady at a restaurant in Ceaser's Palace as Maria began to talk reckless in front of the undercover agent about all her dealings with Anna. As soon as Anna made a proposition for the undercover brunette to work in her brothel back in Texas, she was surrounded by Federal agents. Anna was charged with pimping, pandering and human trafficking.

CHAPTER 21

Six months passed while Anna sat in Pahrump which was at the time the Federal holding facility in Vegas waiting on her trial date with no bond. Luckily for Anna, her money was long enough to still get anything she wanted. She had a cell phone and was still making moves from inside her jail cell between Shorty, The Sophisticats and her out of town buyers. Even her reputation proceeded her. All of the hoes who went inside the Las Vegas jail had heard of the infamous Ms. Anna Davis at some point of their hoing career. Nobody dared to cross her from the horrendous stories they heard about her murder game.

Many of the women who were locked up allowed their appearance to go down while behind bars. Anna refused to be one of them. She worked out every morning doing crunches and jogging until she got a good sweat. She improvised with the items on commissary that she bought to continue to maintain her beauty. She used Kool-Aid packs to rub on her lips for lipstick and bought coloring pencils to melt down and use for eye liner and eye shadow.

She gathered a bunch of tampons and used for curlers to curl her hair when she got out of the shower. The women guards were jealous of Anna and the male guards often tried to flirt with her. One particular night, an older white male guard named Hefty about 45 years old stopped by Anna's cell when all of the inmates were asleep and unlocked her cell. Anna thought she was dreaming when she heard the cell open, but she was awakened as Hefty shined his flashlight into her face.

"Inmate Davis," he whispered. "Come with me."

At first Anna wanted to curse him out for waking her up, but she decided to get up and see what he wanted. When she walked out of the cell she followed him down a hallway as he led her into an empty mop closet.

"What the fuck do you want?" asked Anna.

"You know what I want," he said as he groped her breast and grabbed his dick. "I can't fuck right now. I'm on my period," lied Anna.

"Shit!" said Hefty

"Don't worry. I have something better for you," she said.

Anna got down on her knees and unbuckled Hefty's pants as she began to simultaneously suck his dick and tickle his balls. Hefty was overwhelmed with delight as Anna wrapped her warm mouth around the shaft of his rod and began to deep throat him like a pro. In no time he was erupting like a volcano as Anna purposely caught every drop of his semen on the front of her prison uniform. When Hefty walked her back to her cell, she changed her shirt and neatly folded the cum stained uniform shirt under her mattress for insurance. She now had the leverage that she needed against a Federal government employee she would eventually use to go home.

When Anna finally went to trial, she was sentenced to 27 years Federal for human trafficking. Her lawyers immediately asked to appeal the case hoping that she could win on appeal. After the federal sentence was handed down to Anna, she went back to her cell to lie down in her bunk and reflect on her life.

She wondered how in the hell did she go from being a dumb ass white girl and prostitute to being one of the best pimps in the country? How in the hell did she go from being a pimp into one of the most ruthless and feared drug bosses in the country? How could Maria set her up? Why didn't she kill Maria a long time ago when she found out she was stashing money behind her back? And last but not least, she wondered how in the hell did she go from being a multi-millionaire living in a 6.8 million-dollar mansion to living in a six by nine cell and living out of a locker?

Most importantly, she wondered how in the fuck would she get out because no way in hell would the magnificent Ms. Anna Davis be serving the next 27 years in Federal Prison.

She smiled as she began to remember the cum stained shirt under her mattress. She planned to call her lawyer, first thing in the morning and give him a good story and provide solid evidence on how she was raped by a Federal Corrections officer and demand immunity for immediate release or have him threat to file a civil lawsuit against the Federal Bureau of Prisons and cause a nationwide news story.

Coming Soon
"If These Walls Could Talk
Part 5
REVELATIONS

ABOUT THE AUTHOR

A prolific writer, Ricky St. Julien II also known as the rapper "SILK G" is a native of Orange, Texas who currently resides in Houston, Texas. He began his craft in writing as an independent rap artist and transformed his passion for words and creativity into the form of books.

Besides his most popular self-help book titled "48 Laws of Hustling," he is also the author of many other works which include modern day urban fiction, erotica, poetry and movie scripts. He not only strives to be a bestselling author, but simply the best.

Made in the USA
Columbia, SC
15 June 2025

59426908R00052